ISBN-10: 1541270096

ISBN-13: 978-1541270091

For Kings of Kings and Storm.-M.S.L

For my two total opposites. M.L

All our friends that helped make this possible. M.L

Whistling

Hic, *hic*!

Oh, Boy.

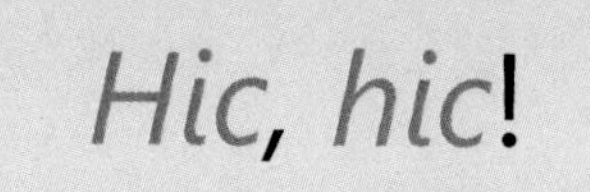
Hic, hic!

Oh no, I caught the hiccups!

Hic, *hic*!

How... *hic, hic*... do I get rid of them?

Pebble soup? *Hic, hic* no.

Cricket ice pop? *Hic, hic* no.

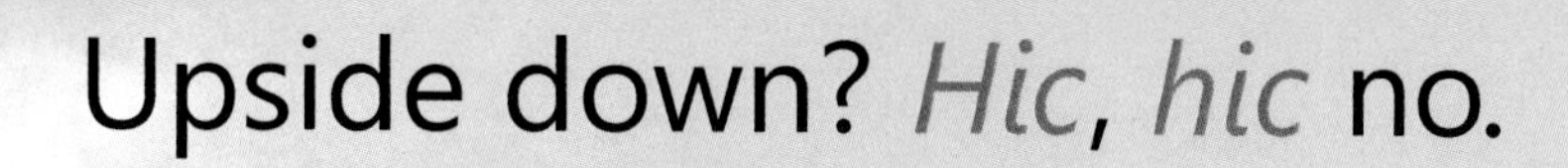
Upside down? *Hic*, *hic* no.

Scary?

Boo!

Ahhhh !

Hic, *hic* no.

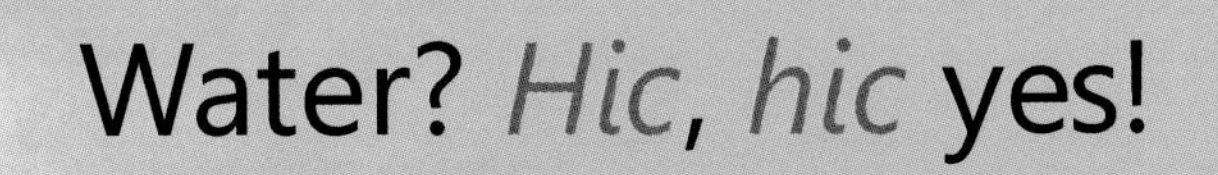
Water? *Hic*, *hic* yes!

Where did...

The water *hic*, *hic*

Go??

Someone moved the river!

Tap, tap

Hic, hic Yes.

Stormee are you ok ?

Ok? I'm not ok, I caught the *hic*, *hic*, hiccups.

Hiccups? How did you get them?

You, Sam.

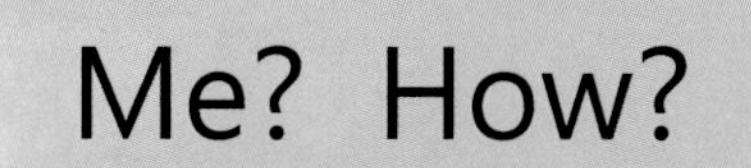
Me? How?

You had them yesterday. *Hic*, *hic* and now I do.

I can show you how I got rid of them.

WATER!

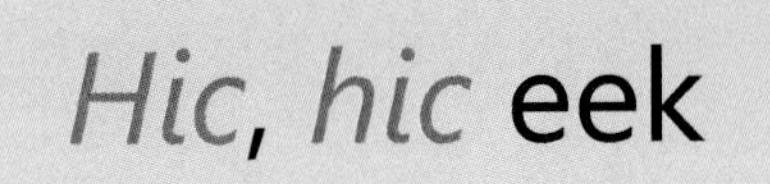
Hic, *hic* eek

Hic, hic Gulp.

Whoosh.

Hic, hic Ahhhh.

Plop.

They're finally gone.

Oh, yeah.

What a beautiful day.

Achoo!

Oh, Boy.

Please look out for the next book *Stormee the Ostrich gets the Achoos!* Coming soon...

Moniqua Lewis is a native of Long Island, New York. She currently resides in Georgia with her family. Stormee the ostrich is modeled after her loving Ridgeback (Storm) and all his crazy adventures.

Michael Lewis enjoys time with his family, watching and occasional sketching for his daughters in his home state of Georgia.

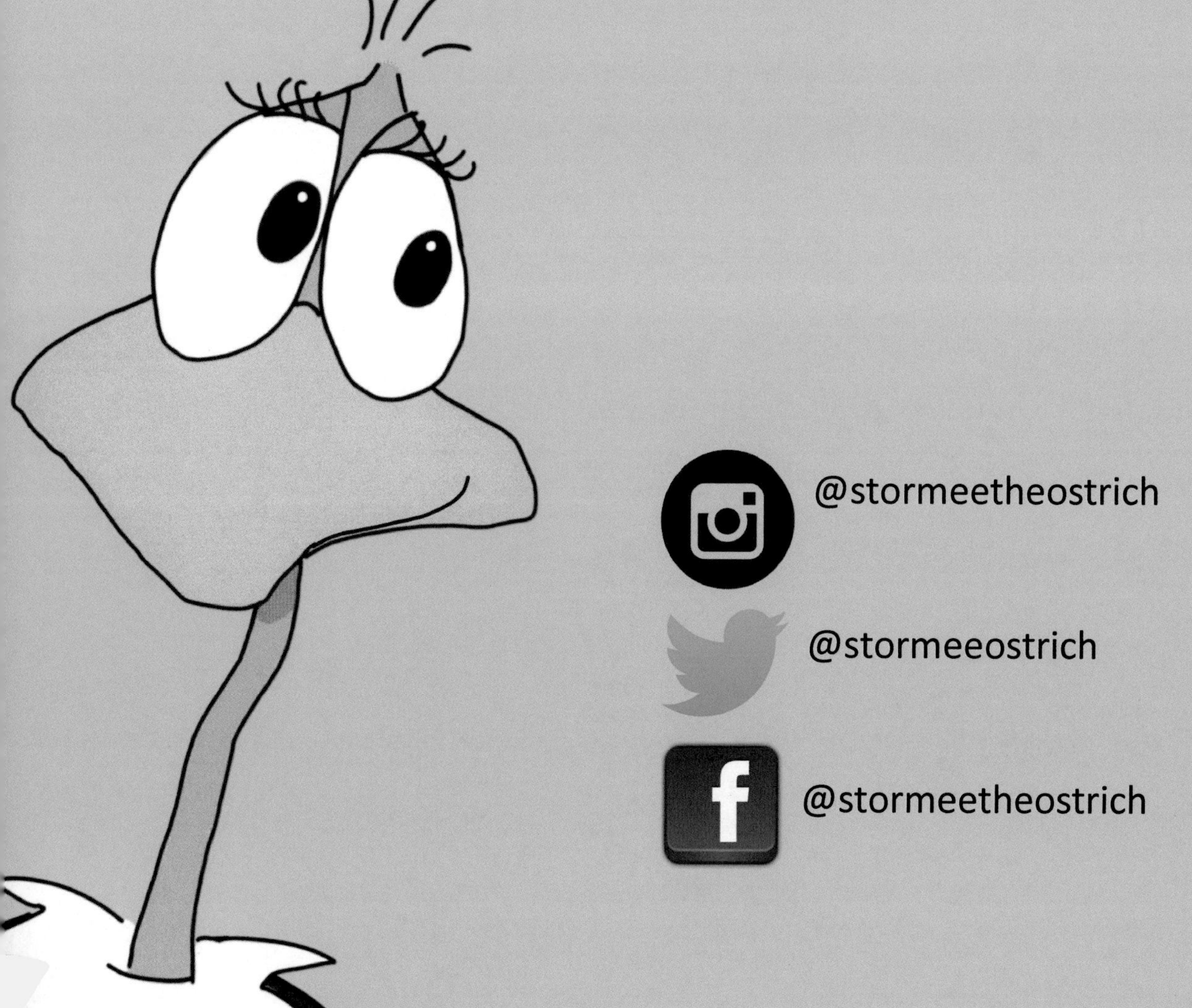

Made in the USA
Middletown, DE
03 December 2019